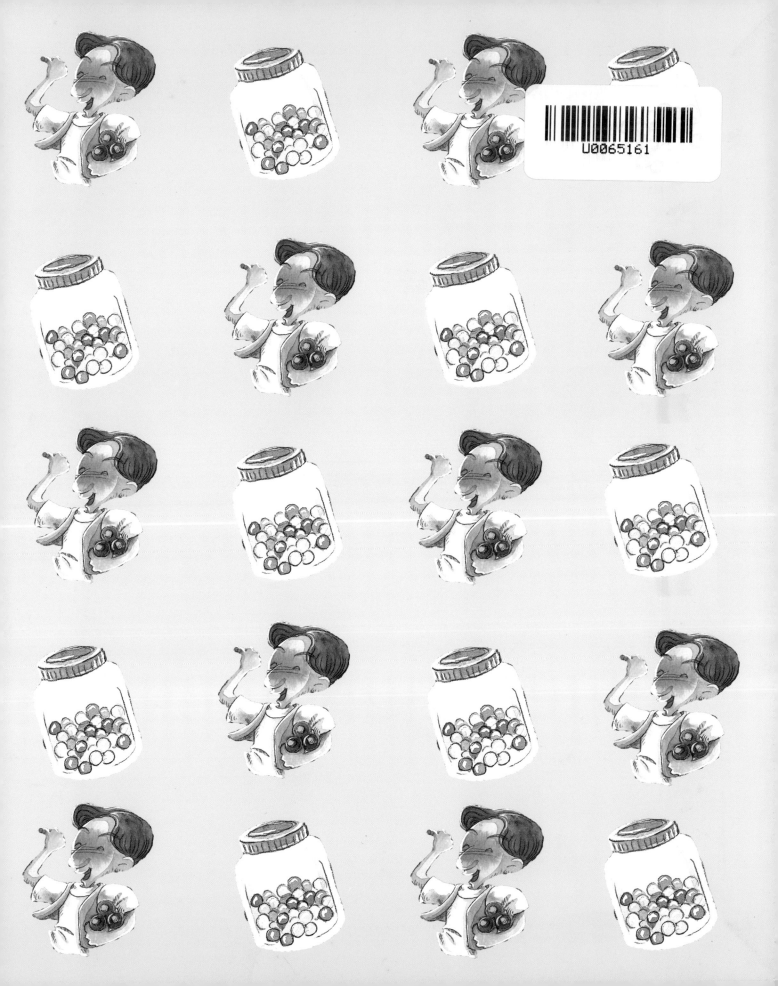

School's Out

耶！放假了！

Coleen Reddy 著

倪靖、郜欣、王平 繪

蘇秋華 譯

三民書局

For Gemk

My Soulmate

獻給我的心靈伴侶——Gemk

Everyone at Dogooder Junior High School was excited. It was the last day of school. Then they would have a summer vacation for two months. At school, everyone talked excitedly about what they would do during the summer vacation.

"I'm going to visit my cousins in New York," said Jason.

"You're lucky," said David. "I'm not going anywhere and my parents want me to get a job."

"I'm going to England for two weeks with my family," said Amy.

"I'm not doing much. I'll probably play computer games and watch lots of movies," said Kyle.

"It's the last day of school," said Amy. "We should celebrate. We should have a party."

"Whose house can we use for a party?" asked David.

"Hey, my parents are going out tonight. They're going to the opera. When they go to the opera, they usually get back very late," said Jason.

"Are you sure your parents won't mind you having a party at your house when they're not there?" asked Amy.

"I won't tell them. They'll never know. We can have the party for a few hours and then everyone can leave before they get home," said Jason.

"That sounds a little dangerous," said Kyle. "What if they get home early and catch us?"

"That won't happen. The opera always finishes very late," said Jason.

"Okay," said Amy. "I'll go to your party. Will you invite any other students?"

"I'll invite about 10 students. I don't want too many people to come," said Jason.

"Sounds like fun," said David. "Count me in."

"Yeah, me too," said Kyle.

That night, at 7:00 the students met at Jason's house. Only five of the students that Jason had invited came to his party. He was a little disappointed. He invited everyone in and told them to sit in the living room.

Everyone just sat there, looking bored.

"I know!" said Jason. "We can dance."

Jason played a CD. The music was very loud. But nobody wanted to dance. Everyone was too shy.

"Jason, do you have anything to eat? I'm starving," said David.

"There's some pizza in the refrigerator," said Jason. Jason and David went to the kitchen to get the pizza. Just then the doorbell rang. Amy answered it. There were about fifteen of Amy's classmates at the door.

"Hello, Amy," said one boy. "We heard there was a party here. Can we come in?"

But before Amy could say anything, they walked past her and into Jason's house.

After that, more and more students started arriving. Pretty soon, Jason's house was crowded with students. Jason didn't even know most of them. They turned up the music and started dancing.

Some of them began dancing on the sofas and tables.
"Oh no!" thought Jason. "How do I get all these people to leave?"

Kyle and David wanted something to drink.

"There's more lemonade in the basement," said Jason.

"Can you guys get it for me?"

"Sure," said David.

David and Kyle went into the basement to look for the lemonade.

"What's this?" Kyle asked.

He found some unlabelled bottles on a shelf.

"I don't know," said David. "Open it."

Kyle opened the bottle.

"Mmm..." said Kyle. "It smells good. It smells like grape juice."

"Let me taste it," said David.

David took a sip.

"It IS grape juice and it's yummy," said David.

"Let me have some; I'm thirsty," said Kyle.

The two boys drank the whole bottle of 'grape juice.'

There were more bottles of the 'grape juice' so they decided to take them upstairs instead of looking for the lemonade.

When they were walking up the stairs, for some reason Kyle and David found it difficult to walk straight.

"I don't feel so good," said Kyle. Then he started giggling.

"Me too," said David. He also started giggling.

They took the bottles of grape juice to Jason.

"This is not the lemonade," said Jason.

"No, it's not. But it's better than lemonade. It's grape juice and it tastes so good that Kyle and I drank a whole bottle," said David. Then he and Kyle burst into a fit of giggles.

"You idiots! This is not grape juice. THIS IS WINE!" yelled Jason. "My father collects this wine. It's from Europe and it's very expensive!"

David and Kyle looked sick. Kyle's face was turning green.
"I don't feel well. I think I'm going to throw up," said Kyle.
Kyle turned to the nearest thing he could find. It was
Jason's mother's expensive Ming vase. Before anyone knew
what was going on, he threw up into the vase.
"No!" yelled Jason.

"What's going on?" asked Amy.

"Kyle and David are DRUNK. They drank my father's wine. They thought it was grape juice," said Jason.

"I think you should send everyone home," said Amy. "Your parents will be home soon."

Jason and Amy went around telling everyone that the party was over. Finally everyone went home except for Amy, and Kyle and David, who were both sleeping upstairs in Jason's bedroom.

Amy helped Jason clean up. Amy
had to wash the vase that Kyle had
thrown up in. Just then, they heard a
car. It was Jason's parents. They
were already home.

"Let's go upstairs quickly!" said Jason.

Amy and Jason ran into Jason's bedroom and closed the door. Kyle and David were still asleep. David was talking in his sleep. He was saying strange things.

"No mom, don't buy me Pikachu underwear," David murmured in his sleep.

Amy and Jason wanted to laugh but they couldn't make a sound. Jason's parents were in the house. They had to be very quiet and wait for Jason's parents to go to bed. Then they could sneak out of the house with Kyle and David.

Finally, Jason's parents went to bed.

Jason and Amy tried to wake Kyle and David up.

"Wake up, David!" said Amy as she shook him.

"Yes, mommy," said David.

Amy and Jason wanted to laugh but they were afraid that any noise would wake Jason's parents up.

After a few minutes, David and Kyle were still half asleep but Amy and Jason led them down the stairs and out of the house.

David and Kyle still weren't fully awake. In fact, once they were outside, they started sleeping on the lawn.

"Let's turn the garden hose on and spray them with cold water. That should wake them up," said Jason.

Jason went away for a few minutes and returned with a hose that his dad used for watering the garden.

He turned it on and sprayed David and Kyle with water.
Both David and Kyle immediately woke up and screamed.
"What's going on?" yelled David.
"You guys wouldn't wake up because you drank so much wine," said Amy.

Then Kyle started laughing. He pulled the hose away from Jason and sprayed him and Amy.

Pretty soon, they were all laughing and having the best water fight.

They were happy as they celebrated the start of summer vacation.

Upstairs, in Jason's room, his father looked out of the window after hearing strange sounds in his garden. He saw his son and three of his best friends having the time of their lives. He smiled and went back to bed.

耶！放假了！

督顧德國中所有學生都很興奮，因為今天是本學期的最後一天，從明天起，他們便要開始放長達兩個月的暑假了！學校裡，大家都興高采烈地討論著暑期計畫。

杰生說：「我要到紐約去看我的表哥和表弟。」

大維很羨慕地說：「你真好命，我哪兒都不能去，而且我爸媽還要我去找工作。」

愛玫說：「我們全家要去英國兩個禮拜。」

凱爾則說：「我沒有什麼事好做。我想我可能會玩電動，看一堆電影來打發時間吧。」

愛玫提議：「今天是學期末，應該好好慶祝，乾脆我們來辦個派對，你們覺得怎樣？」

大維問：「那誰家可以讓我們開派對呢？」

杰生說：「對了，我爸媽今天晚上要去聽歌劇，不在家。每次他們去聽歌劇都會很晚才回來。」

愛玫覺得不是很放心：「你確定你爸媽不會介意我們趁他們不在的時候開派對嗎？」

(p.1〜p.5)

杰生說：「反正我不跟他們講，他們也不會知道。我們可以玩幾個小時，然後在他們回來以前請大家回家。」

凱爾說：「聽起來不是很保險，萬一他們提早回來，我們被逮個正著怎麼辦？」

杰生說：「絕對不會發生這種事的。歌劇都很晚才散場。」

愛玫說：「好吧，我參加。你還會不會邀其他人去啊？」

杰生想了想：「我大概會邀請十個人左右，我不希望太多的人來。」

大維附和：「好像很好玩，也算我一份。」

晚上七點，同學們來到杰生家會合。杰生邀請的人當中，一共只來了五個，杰生覺得有點失望。他請朋友到客廳「坐」，然後大家就只是「坐」在沙發上，看起來一副很無聊的樣子。

(p.5～p.9)

杰生想到一個點子：「對了，我們可以跳舞啊。」

於是他開始放瑞奇・馬汀的 CD，音樂開得震天價響，可是卻沒有一個人想跳舞，大家都太內向了。

大維說：「杰生，你家有沒有吃的，我快餓死了。」

杰生說：「冰箱裡還有一點披薩。」

就在杰生和大維到廚房拿披薩時，門鈴響了，愛玫便去開門，來的是愛玫的同學，大約有十五個人。

其中一個男孩子對愛玫說：「哈囉，我們聽說這裡有派對，可以參加嗎？」愛玫還來不及回答，他們就自行進屋了。

之後，來了愈來愈多的同學，很快地，杰生家便擠滿了人，大部份的人杰生根本不認識。他們把音樂調得超大聲，然後跳起舞來，有些人跳一跳甚至跳到沙發和桌上。

杰生心想：「不好了，我要怎樣才能叫他們回家呢？」

（p.9～p.13）

凱爾和大維想喝點飲料。

杰生說：「地下室還有檸檬汁。你們可以順便幫我拿上來嗎？」

大維應了聲「當然」，就和凱爾一起到地下室找檸檬汁。

凱爾找到一瓶沒有標籤的瓶子，問：「這是什麼？」

大維說：「我也不曉得，打開看看。」

凱爾打開瓶蓋，聞了聞，說：「嗯……還蠻好聞的，好像是葡萄汁。」

大維說：「我喝喝看。」於是便啜飲了一小口。

他說：「是葡萄汁，而且很好喝。」

凱爾說：「我也要喝，我快渴死了。」

於是這兩個人便把一整瓶的「葡萄汁」解決了。

他們看到還有好幾瓶葡萄汁，便決定把它們通通搬上樓，不再找什麼檸檬汁了。

爬樓梯的時候，不知因為什麼緣故，凱爾和大維覺得沒辦法走成一直線。

凱爾說：「我覺得不太舒服。」然後就咯咯笑了起來。

大維附和他的話：「我也是。」他也咯咯笑了。

他們一起把葡萄汁拿給杰生。

(p.14～p.19)

杰生看了看瓶子，說：「這不是檸檬汁。」

大維說：「不是，可是比檸檬汁還好喝，這種葡萄汁好喝得不得了，所以我和凱爾喝了一整瓶。」說完，他和凱爾竟然不約而同爆出一串笑聲。

杰生氣得大喊：「你們兩個是白痴啊？這不是葡萄『汁』，是葡萄『酒』！我爸爸有收藏葡萄酒的習慣，這些酒是從歐洲帶回來的，而且很貴！」

大維和凱爾臉色很難看，凱爾甚至臉色發青。

凱爾說：「我覺得很難過，我想吐。」

話才說完，他就轉向最靠近他身邊的東西——剛好是杰生媽媽那只很昂貴的明朝花瓶。其他人還來不及反應，凱爾就嘩啦嘩啦地吐到花瓶裡。

杰生慘叫：「噢！不！」

愛玫說：「怎麼啦！發生什麼事了？」

杰生回答她：「凱爾和大維喝醉了，他們把我爸爸的酒當成葡萄汁喝光了。」

愛玫說：「我想你爸媽應該快回來了，你得快請大家回家。」

（p.19～p.22）

杰生和愛玫一一向客廳裡的人說派對結束了，請趕快回家。最後好不容易把所有人都打發了，只剩下愛玫、凱爾，和大維。兩個男孩在樓上杰生的房裡呼呼大睡，愛玫和杰生則在樓下收拾殘局。愛玫得把凱爾吐過的花瓶沖洗乾淨。就在這個時候，他們聽到汽車的聲音，杰生的爸媽回來了。

杰生說：「趕快躲到樓上去。」

他們兩個一起衝到杰生房裡，把門關上。凱爾和大維還是睡得很沈，大維甚至說起奇怪的夢話，睡夢中，他咕噥著：「不要，媽，不要幫我買皮卡丘的內褲啦。」

愛玫和杰生聽了很想笑，可是卻不能笑出聲音來，因為杰生的爸媽就在樓下。他們得保持安靜，等到杰生的父母都睡了，才能帶凱爾和大維一起溜出去。

（p.23～p.26）

總算等到杰生的爸媽上床睡了，杰生和愛玫努力地想把凱爾和大維弄醒。

愛玫一邊搖晃大維，一邊說：「大維，醒醒啊！」

大維卻回答：「好啦，媽媽。」

愛玫和杰生都覺得好笑，可是又怕笑太大聲會吵醒杰生的爸媽。

幾分鐘後，大維和凱爾雖然還在半睡半醒當中，卻在愛玫和杰生的帶領下，下樓走到屋外。

大維和凱爾還沒有完全醒過來，事實上，他們一走到屋外，便繼續躺在草坪上呼呼大睡。

杰生提議：「把冷水灑在他們身上，這樣應該叫得醒他們。」

他離開了一會兒，回來時，手上拿著一條他爸爸平時用來澆花的水管。

（p.27～p.30）

他扭開水龍頭，把水管對準大維和凱爾噴水。

大維和凱爾立刻醒了過來，大聲尖叫。

大維大吼：「發生什麼事了？」

愛玫說：「你們酒喝太多了，怎樣都叫不醒。」

凱爾笑了出來，一把搶過水管，對準杰生和愛玫猛噴水。

很快地，他們四個就邊笑鬧，邊打起一場最過癮的水仗來了。

四個人歡欣鼓舞地慶祝暑假的到來。

杰生的爸爸由於聽到花園裡有奇怪的聲音，便來到樓上杰生的房裡，從窗口張望。

看到自己的兒子和三個好朋友玩得很開心，他發出會心的一笑，便靜靜回房休息了。

（p.31～p.35）

國家圖書館出版品預行編目資料

School's Out:耶！放假了！ ／Coleen Reddy著；倪靖,
郜欣, 王平繪；蘇秋華譯.－－初版一刷.－－臺北
市；三民，2002
　　面；公分－－(愛閱雙語叢書. 青春記事簿系列)
中英對照
ISBN 957-14-3662-3　（平裝）

805

© School's Out
——耶！放假了！

著作人　Coleen Reddy
繪　圖　倪靖　郜欣　王平
譯　者　蘇秋華
發行人　劉振強
著作財
產權人　三民書局股份有限公司
　　　　臺北市復興北路三八六號
發行所　三民書局股份有限公司
　　　　地址／臺北市復興北路三八六號
　　　　電話／二五〇〇六六〇〇
　　　　郵撥／〇〇〇九九九八——五號
印刷所　三民書局股份有限公司
門市部　復北店／臺北市復興北路三八六號
　　　　重南店／臺北市重慶南路一段六十一號
初版一刷　西元二〇〇二年十一月
編　號　S 85623
定　價　新臺幣參佰伍拾元整
行政院新聞局登記證局版臺業字第〇二〇〇號